D0968833

# Marla's
# Toyshop Adventure

by Andy Rector
Illustrated by Tim Bowers

Marla Mouse was trying to sleep. "What is all that noise?" she said. "I can't sleep."

Marla opened her front door. She saw elves everywhere!

The elves hammered nails into wood. They dropped paint cans on the floor with a thud. They talked and talked with excitement in their voices. No wonder Marla could not sleep!

Marla watched them all
evening. Finally the elves
left their toyshop. All the
toys were made.

The elves had made
many toys! Marla walked
out of her mouse hole.
She wanted to explore.

Marla found a top. She spun it. She found another top. She spun it, too. She found a third top. She spun it, too. She had three tops spinning at once.

Marla found a tea
set. She had tea with
the Queen.

Marla played electronic
football. She danced
on the buttons and made
a touchdown.

What was that noise?
thought Marla. She
looked around. A cat!
Marla jumped into a toy
car and drove away.

Marla escaped into a big doll house. In the bedroom she found a bed. She slept safely in a doll bed hidden from the cat.

The next morning Marla woke up and heard a voice. "Someone has been playing with the toys!" Marla ran out of the doll house. She saw Santa Claus. "Santa," said Marla. "Let me help you give these toys to children. I want them to have as much fun as I did."

That night was Christmas
Eve. The Elves packed
Santa's toy bag. Santa
Claus and Marla rode
all night giving toys to
children all over the world.
Marla never forgot that
wonderful Christmas!